For the giants

Originally published in French under the title *L'autobus* by Comme des géants inc.

Copyright © 2014 Marianne Dubuc
Copyright © 2014 Comme des géants inc.
Translation rights arranged through VeroK Agency, Spain

English translation © 2015 Kids Can Press

Kids Can Press acknowledges the financial support of the Government of Ontario, through the Ontario Media Development Corporation's Ontario Book Initiative.

Published in Canada by
Kids Can Press Ltd.
25 Dockside Drive
Toronto, ON M5A 0B5

Published in the U.S. by
Kids Can Press Ltd.
2250 Military Road
Tonawanda, NY 14150

www.kidscanpress.com

Original edition edited by Nadine Robert and Mathieu Lavoie
English edition edited by Yvette Ghione
Designed by Mathieu Lavoie

Manufactured in Shenzhen, Guang Dong, P.R. China, in 10/2014 by Printplus Limited

CM 15 0 9 8 7 6 5 4 3 2 1

Library and Archives Canada Cataloguing in Publication

Dubuc, Marianne, 1980–
[Autobus. English]
     The bus ride / Marianne Dubuc.
Translation of: L'autobus.
English translation by Yvette Ghione.
ISBN 978-1-77138-209-0 (bound)
     I. Ghione, Yvette, translator II. Title. III. Title: Autobus.
English.
PS8607.U2245A9713 2014   jC843'.6   C2014-903115-7

Kids Can Press is a *Corus*™ Entertainment company

THE BUS RIDE

MARIANNE DUBUC

Kids Can Press

"Bye, Mom! Yes, I know! I'll be good."

This is the first time I'm taking the bus by myself.

Mom packed me a snack — and had me bring my sweater in case I get cold.

But I won't get cold. I never do.

I wonder how many stops the bus will make. Maybe I'll count them …

"Oh! What pretty flowers! Thank you very much, Miss."

Look — we're riding through the forest.

That little wolf looks friendly.

Luckily, Mom packed two cookies.

I love shortbread.

Yikes! I can't see a thing!

Who turned out the lights?

Something isn't quite right ...

How did I get *here*?! And where's my cookie?

That's more like it.

"Bye, little wolf! Don't forget — I live in the house on the right side of the road, just past the big oak tree."

I wonder what's in that giant box ...

Oh, no! A thief!

Stealing is wrong.

Everyone knows that.

We scared him off!

It's too bad I don't have any more cookies to share.

Rats! I forgot to count how many stops we've made so far.

This neighborhood looks familiar. It shouldn't be too much farther.

Gee, he's had a really long nap.

My stop is next. Do I have everything? Yes — my basket, my sweater.

"Grandma! Grandma!"

"Grandma! Grandma!"

"I'm here!"

"I have so much to tell you …"